S0-AFN-917

JOANIE
Cartoons for New Children by G.B. Trudeau

Ms. Joanie Caucus, the middle-aged mentor of Walden Commune, is perhaps the only feminist character in daily syndication to be hailed wholeheartedly by the women's movement. Appearing in Garry Trudeau's comic strip, "DOONESBURY," Joanie and her precocious charges at the day-care center have, over the last several years, provided amusement and enlightenment on a vital topic which is chronically misrepresented. Joanie has become at once a wise and sensitive spokeswoman for the movement, and in this volume she provides a humanist point of reference for free children still in the vulnerable process of assimilating roles in a changing society.

CARTOONS FOR NEW CHILDREN

The books in this series are designed to stimulate children into asking questions and to invite child and parent alike to examine often confusing contemporary problems from fresh perspectives. Parents are encouraged by the Afterword in each book to challenge the validity and honesty of their own beliefs in preparing their children to face a changing society. Children today are exposed to the problems of their world at a much earlier age than any previous generation; the "Cartoons for New Children Series" can provide gentle access to a mutual understanding between those who are curious and those who must show the way.

JOANIE

CARTOONS
FOR NEW CHILDREN

A Doonesbury Book
by Garry Trudeau

With an Afterword
for Parents and Teachers
by Nora Ephron

RL 4, IL 4-up

JOANIE
*A Bantam Book / published by arrangement with
Andrews & McMeel, Inc.*

PRINTING HISTORY
Andrews & McMeel edition published November 1974
1st printing .... December 1974   2nd printing ... December 1974
3rd printing ..... March 1975
Bantam edition / July 1979

All rights reserved.
Copyright © 1974 by G.B. Trudeau
*This book may not be reproduced in whole or in part, by
mimeograph or any other means, without permission.
For information address: Andrews & McMeel, Inc.
6700 Squibb Road, Mission, Kansas 66202*

ISBN 0-553-10296-6

Published simultaneously in the United States and Canada

Bantam Books are published by Bantam Books, Inc.
Its trademark, consisting of the words "Bantam Books"and
the portrayal of a bantam, is Registered in U.S. Patent and
Trademark Office and in other countries. Marca Registrada. Bantam
Books, Inc., 666 Fifth Avenue, New York, New York 10019.

PRINTED IN THE UNITED STATES OF AMERICA

0 9 8 7 6 5 4 3 2

To Lynton

GROWING UP TO BE A MOMMY IS ONE OF THE MOST WONDERFUL THINGS A LITTLE GIRL CAN WANT TO DO. BUT — THERE ARE OTHER THINGS IN LIFE SHE CAN DO AS WELL..

FOR INSTANCE, SHE CAN WORK HER HEAD OFF AND SHOW ALL THOSE ARROGANT BOYS THAT SHE'S JUST AS CAPABLE AND INTELLIGENT AS ANY LITTLE STUD AROUND!!

OKAY, I GUESS—SHE'S BEEN ADMINISTERING CONSCIOUSNESS RAISING SESSIONS TO THE GIRLS...

TERRIFIC!

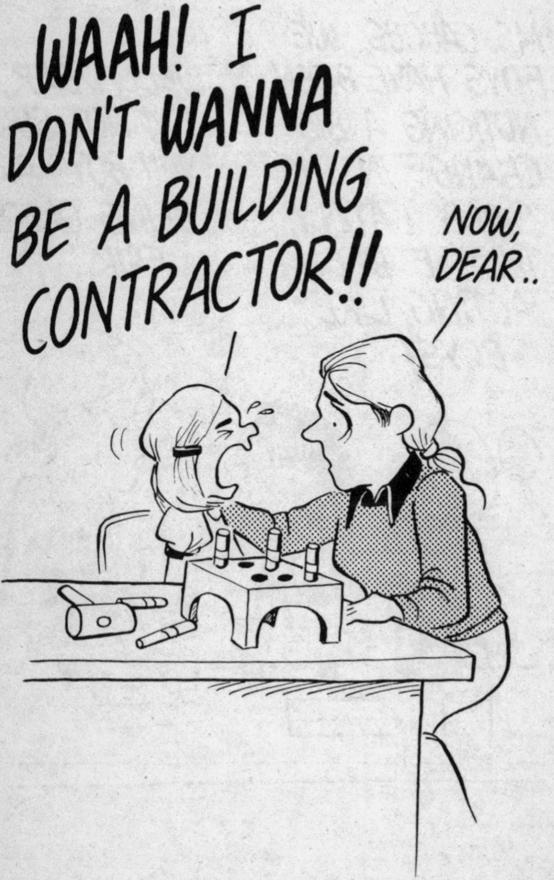
WAAH! I DON'T WANNA BE A BUILDING CONTRACTOR!!
NOW, DEAR..

MS. CAUCUS, WE BOYS HAVE BEEN NOTICING A BIG CHANGE IN THE GIRLS LATELY. THEY'VE BEEN ACTING LIKE BOYS!
WELL, DEAR, I'M NOT SURE YOU BOYS ARE BEING QUITE FAIR..

A GREAT LADY, SIMONE DE BEAUVOIR, ONCE SAID THAT THERE ARE TWO KINDS OF PEOPLE — HUMAN BEINGS AND WOMEN. BUT WHEN WOMEN START ACTING LIKE HUMAN BEINGS, THEY ARE ACCUSED OF TRYING TO BE LIKE MEN.

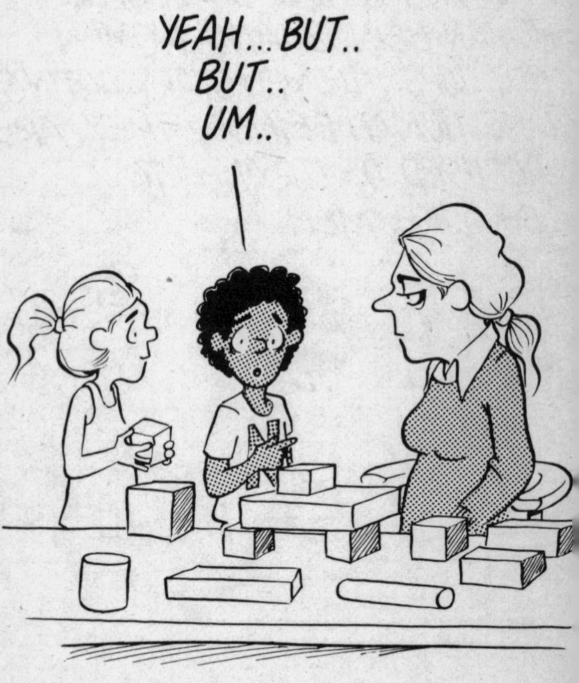
YEAH... BUT..
BUT..
UM..

SIMONE DE BEAUVOIR'S GOT YOUR NUMBER, SLIM.

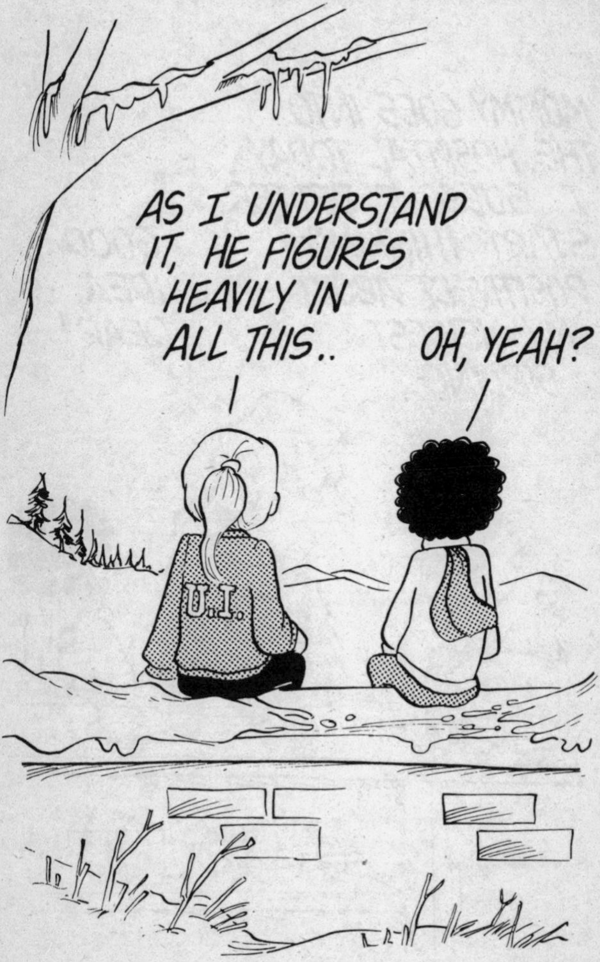
AS I UNDERSTAND IT, HE FIGURES HEAVILY IN ALL THIS..
OH, YEAH?

WHO'S THIS?.. ZONKER? HI, KIDDO- IT'S JOANIE. SAY, WHO'S MAKING DINNER TONIGHT? DO YOU KNOW?..
DOUBLE FAULT!
HEE! HEE!
OL
4+2

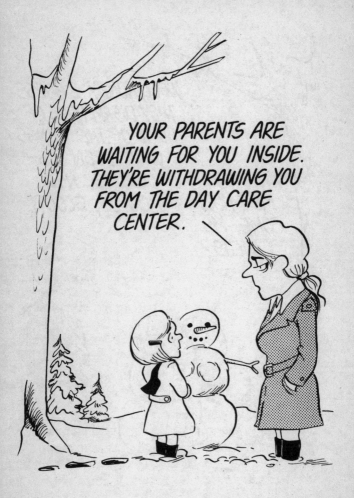

AFTERWORD
FOR PARENTS AND TEACHERS
By Nora Ephron

I live in a city that has only a few major failings—and one of them is that there are no newspapers that carry "Doonesbury" in their comics sections. So I came late to Garry Trudeau and his characters, heard about them at a party in Washington, when a woman friend told me all about someone named Joanie Caucus. Ms. Caucus. I sat through the conversation smiling patiently, humoring my friend, because I did not believe her. Joanie Caucus, she told me, was funny. Genuinely funny. It seemed to me that the likelihood of that was next to impossible. I should point out that I am not one of those who believe that there is nothing to laugh at about the women's movement; in fact, there is plenty to laugh about without in any way putting down the movement, and I become downright irritable when I read lengthy feminist tracts justifying the women's movement's lack of sense of humor. "How can we laugh when we're so oppressed?" That kind of thing. It seems to me that the exact opposite is true: how can we *not* laugh when we're so oppressed. In spite of what I feel about the women's movement, in spite of the huge role it has played in my life, there are aspects of it that are just plain funny. Not at the time. I have to say that. But afterward, when I think that I spent days, weeks even, discussing who was going to sort the socks, *his* socks—well, you get the picture.

In any case, the women's movement has spawned very little humor—much less any humor that amuses me. And Joanie Caucus hardly seemed a likely candidate; she was, after all, the creation of a man. Then I started reading "Doonesbury," and there was Joanie, the runaway wife, the day-care center supervisor, the law school applicant, the newly-single woman coping with passes from a hip priest with hot tickets to a Jeb Magruder concert, and I began to roar.

There is nothing more hopeless than attempting to explain why something is funny. Once, in the course of a checkered newspaper career, I had to read excerpts from a college thesis on humor by Johnny Carson; he took a series of absolutely hilarious jokes by Jack Benny and Fred Allen and rendered them utterly stultifying with his long-winded analyses of what made them work. I don't want to do that to Joanie. For one thing, I am a little in love with her. For another, I have no idea why she is funny. I just know she kills me. And I think about her all the time. It's not just that I know women like her and that I'm a little like her myself. It's not just that my friends constantly tell me stories about trying to bring the movement to their children, stories that are remarkably like the episodes in this book. It's also that there is something about what she looks like and the way she behaves—so downtrodden and yet plucky, so saggy and yet upright, so droopy-eyed and yet wide a-wake, so pessimistic and yet deep-down slyly sure that she's on the right track. I don't want to take this too seriously, but she seems such a perfect, sympathetic mirror-image of all of us who are trying to make sense out of the contradictions, trying to assimilite all the new information and ideas and theories into our messy lives and minds. It's not easy, folks—and I love that Joanie makes it look

so hard. It's occasionally absurd and ridiculous—
and I love that she makes it look so funny. It seems
to me that this book provides a perfect, absolutely
painless way for parents to introduce some of
these ideas to their children.

I got to the end of this lovely book, to the strip
where Joanie tells Mary that her parents are with-
drawing her from the day-care center: Joanie with
her false bravado, her "scoot" to cover her feel-
ings. And Mary, who is smarter than the rest of us,
knows that it is she who must offer the reassur-
ance. "Hang in there, sister!" she says. And
Joanie's mouth snakes upward, in that deliciously
wicked way it tends to. "I will, dear," she says.

God, it's wonderful.